# PRAISE FOR IMAGINE... THE GREAT FLOOD

"I couldn't be more proud of Guild alum, Matt Koceich! He had a dream, persevered, and would not be denied. Enjoy this result, and may it be only the first of many."

—Jerry Jenkins, Novelist & Biographer, Owner, The Jerry Jenkins Writers Guild

"Matt Koceich's *Imagine. . .The Great Flood* is some of the best biblical historical fiction I've read. The story takes us from modern-day America to Ancient Mesopotamia. . .and ties together neatly the link between faith in God and trust in people we love, regardless of apparent circumstance. I look forward to the next installment."

—Kaci Hill, screenplay writer and Ted Dekker's coauthor of *Lunatic* and *Elyon*

"Matt Koceich does a masterful job of lifting readers out of the boredom of everyday life, dropping them head-first into a fast-paced, action-packed world of Bible adventure."

—Phil A. Smouse, author and illustrator of over fifty books for kids including *Jesus Wants All of Me*, the children's adaptation of Oswald Chambers' classic devotional, *My Utmost for His Highest*

"*Imagine. . .The Great Flood* is nonstop action in an epic Bible adventure! A well-known story like Noah's Ark comes to life through the eyes of 10-year-old Corey Max with all the wonder of God's creation and the evil forces that want to stop God's plans. (Spoiler alert: God wins!) Boys and girls who like the *I Survived* books will love this action-packed tale."

—Annie Tipton, author of the Diary of a Real Payne series, including the award-winning title *True Story*

# IMAGINE

## *THE GREAT FLOOD*

Matt
Koceich

BARBOUR BOOKS

An Imprint of Barbour Publishing, Inc.

Scripture taken from the HOLY BIBLE, NEW INTERNATIONAL VERSION®, NIV®. Copyright © 1973, 1978, 1984, 2011 by Biblica, Inc.™ Used by permission. All rights reserved worldwide.

Cover illustration: Simon Mendez

Published by Barbour Books, an imprint of Barbour Publishing, Inc., P.O. Box 719, Uhrichsville, Ohio 44683, www.barbourbooks.com

*Our mission is to publish and distribute inspirational products offering exceptional value and biblical encouragement to the masses.*

Member of the
Evangelical Christian
Publishers Association

Printed in the United States of America.

05792   0717   BP

# THOUSANDS OF YEARS AGO

The ocean swirled around the boy and pulled him down with unrelenting power. Heavy water churned and tugged at his flailing body like unseen hands yanking him into the watery depths. The fight was finally over. Even though he'd tried to stand up to the enemy, the waves were about to swallow him whole.

Only minutes before, ten-year-old Corey Max had been standing on the side of a hill high over the valley's edge. After a futile struggle with a vicious giant bent on destruction, Corey couldn't hold on anymore. He'd gripped the staff he'd been given and felt the superhuman pick him up and toss him into the raging sea.

His body had hit the crashing waves.

It felt like he had hit a brick wall.

Back up on the hill, hundreds of local villagers had gathered to watch the unmatched boy battle the superhuman man. They joined the giant in cheering for Corey's demise.

And now, in the clutches of the churning water, the boy was fighting a new battle. He was fighting for his life.

# CHAPTER 1

## PRESENT DAY

### TEXAS

Corey held Molly's leash with a firm grip as his German shepherd pulled him down the sidewalk. Corey's mother alternated between a skip and a slow jog to keep up with both son and dog. Good thing the park was only a block away.

Corey turned around and stared at the eighteen-wheeler parked in front of their house.

It represented everything that was making Corey upset. *New city. New school. New everything*. He turned back and tried to seem upbeat, but his mother caught the sadness etched onto Corey's face.

"Son, I think it's time you try to understand where your father is coming from."

Clouds darkened overhead, even though it hadn't

rained in weeks. Molly pulled against the leash, harder now. The dog couldn't wait to play catch.

"Mom, I've had the same friends for the last seven years. I don't understand why Dad can't find another job here. Why Florida?"

For the past two months, Corey couldn't stop replaying the scene when his father had come home from work and dropped the bomb. He made it sound like Corey and his mother had a say in the decision, but that really wasn't the case. Truth was, the Max family was headed to a new place and leaving everything familiar behind.

"Now Corey, be honest. Our new home is one block from the beach. Clearwater is beautiful. And we'll make sure we go to Disney World over the summers. Can't beat that!"

The neighborhood park came into view. A green plastic slide and three swings with black rubber seats rose up from a circular pit of mulch chips.

Corey didn't respond to his mother's comment. Instead, he unhooked Molly's leash from her collar and told the dog to fly and be free. He thought if he were the dog, maybe the move wouldn't be so bad. Molly didn't have friends to miss and never see again. If only he could be like the dog and just eat and sleep.

"Yes, Mom, the beach sounds cool. But, we've got Galveston here. And Disney World sounds even cooler, but that place is ex-pen-*sive*."

Mom smiled. "You're sounding like a grown-up. Since when did you start worrying about finances?"

Molly was sniffing the grass around the swings, lost in her own world of doggy smells.

Corey ignored his mother's question. "Mom, can you honestly tell me that you want to leave here and move halfway across the country?"

"Well," she said, "sometimes things change. But God never changes, so we rely on Him."

Corey wanted to believe what his mother was saying. He'd heard the Bible stories. He'd read them, too. David and Goliath. Moses and the Pharaoh. Noah and the ark.

Now he would be able to write his own story: *Corey and the Move*.

"Are you listening, son?"

"Yes, ma'am." Listening and understanding were totally different things, though. Corey heard his mother's words, but believing that God was in control of everything was something entirely opposite of hearing.

Molly finished her canine investigations. She returned to Corey's feet. Time for fetching. Corey took a tennis ball from his pocket and tossed it over the swing set. The dog took off like a bolt of lightning. Once the ball was securely trapped in the dog's slobbery mouth, Molly returned it to Corey for another round.

"Corey, sometimes God calls us to places even though we aren't sure what will happen when we get there."

Corey yanked the ball from Molly's mouth and threw it farther this time. It landed by the tree line. The faint sound of thunder echoed in the distance. Molly stopped in her tracks and turned to look at Corey.

"It's okay. Get the ball, girl!"

Corey's voice reassured the dog. Molly snatched her target and brought it back to him. This time his mother reached for the ball.

"Corey, I love you. I'm sorry this move is scary. We're all wondering how it's going to work out. But, what I do know is that God's in charge."

Corey's mother launched the ball, sending the shepherd off on another mission.

Watching his dog run toward the unknown darkness of the woods without a care in the world made Corey see a connection to his own situation.

"Molly trusts us."

The dog disappeared into the trees.

A flash of lightning arced across the sky. Thunder boomed in the distance.

"Yes, honey. She does. We need to do the same thing with God. We need to trust Him with the move. He knows where we're going. He goes before us. God's not going to let us go alone."

Another round of thunder and lightning ripped through the clouds.

Molly, still in the woods, started barking.

"I'll get her," Corey said.

"Hurry! We need to get back before the flood hits."

Corey gave his mom the thumbs-up sign, knowing that Texas storms did come in biblical proportions. He ran after Molly. Her barking got louder the closer he got to the trees. Something was bothering the dog.

Just as Corey reached the woods, he jumped to avoid a log. His right foot caught on the bark, sending him facedown on the ground. Corey's head hit something hard. Pain stabbed behind his eyes, like bolts of lightning.

Molly's barking got louder and more intense.

Corey blinked and tried to get his bearings.

Molly was about twenty feet deeper into the woods. It looked she was barking at someone.

"Molly, come here, girl!"

But the dog kept barking.

Corey couldn't tell if the person was a man or a woman, or if anyone was there at all. It was most likely just his eyes playing tricks because of the fall.

"Molly! Come on!"

Rain started dropping through the treetops and splattered over Corey. He turned and saw his mother coming to help. He tried to get up, but his legs didn't obey his brain.

"Open his eyes," was the last thing Corey thought he heard before the world as he knew it disappeared.

# CHAPTER 2

## 2400 B.C.

### MESOPOTAMIA

It was like an invisible hand pulled back the woods from around Corey. The trees and park were like wrapping paper being ripped away to reveal a gift underneath. The world Corey knew was gone. Molly and his mother just disappeared.

What happened next would be something Corey could never explain. For when the woods were pulled back, an entirely different scene took their place.

In a blink of an eye, the ground underneath Corey's feet changed from leaves, twigs, and branches to gravel. He looked down and saw that he was standing on the side of a hill. The sky here in this new place was crystal clear, and a brilliant yellow-orange sun lit up the land.

Corey turned around, trying to find where his mother

and Molly went. *What just happened?*

"Mom? MOLLY?"

Corey couldn't run through the trees to find his mother because there were none. He turned around in a complete circle. His mother had vanished. Wherever Corey was now, it wasn't in the Texas park. Tendrils of panic began to creep their way through Corey's brain. How was he going to find his mother?

He didn't have time to worry for long. When Corey turned in a circle a second time, he saw a lion standing in front of him. A real, huge lion. The last time Corey was this close to a wild animal was at the Fort Worth Zoo, and there was a thick glass barrier between them.

The majestic beast considered Corey and padded closer.

Corey turned to run but found a second lion staring at him! This one didn't have the flowing mane. Female. She inched closer, her dark eyes fixed on her prey.

Corey was trapped between two vicious beasts. He didn't want to die out here. Wherever "here" was. Corey closed his eyes and asked God for mercy as he waited to be devoured.

"They won't hurt you."

Corey opened his eyes and saw a man with brown skin and a thick black beard standing next to the male lion. He wore a robe like Obi-Wan Kenobi. He held a shepherd's staff in his right hand and a long leather strap in the other.

"He's gentle."

Corey felt fur rub against his leg. He tried to scream, but his mouth wouldn't open. He looked down and saw the male lion was now rubbing his side against Corey's leg, like a child seeking affection.

"See, I told you. They're harmless," the stranger said. "As long as I hold this staff, the animals obey."

Corey had to get out of here and find his mother. "Do you know where my mom is? She has brown hair that comes down to her shoulders. She's wearing a pink shirt and jeans."

"No, but my name is Shem. And you are?"

"Corey. Corey Max. Where are we? How come the lions aren't eating us?"

"Coreymax, things are different here."

"Uh, just Corey. Just call me Core-y."

The man with the odd name considered his request. "Okay, Core-y. Will you help me get these two creatures onto my father's ark?" Shem pointed toward the horizon.

*Unreal.*

The hill they were on ran down into a wide-open plain where a massive wooden boat loomed over the landscape. The wooden structure had to be at least two football fields long and at least five stories tall.

"That looks like Noah's ark," Corey said.

"It *is* Noah's ark. Do you know my father?" Shem asked.

"Yes. Well, no not really. I know *of* him."

Shem just smiled like this was the first time he had heard what Corey said. "Okay, here. Take this and help me get these lions onto the ark." The man handed Corey the leather strap. It turned out to be a primitive leash that resembled a belt. "Loop it around her neck."

Corey wrapped the strap around the female lion's neck. He was blown away that the wild cat didn't move or resist. Corey also realized he wasn't afraid anymore. He missed his mother and Molly. He wanted to know they were okay, but something about the man named Shem and the lions made Corey feel strangely peaceful.

"Come on, Corey." Shem was using his staff to nudge the male lion along.

As they made their way down the rocky outcropping, Corey couldn't believe the lions followed them without resisting. They obeyed like this was the way things were supposed to be.

After a handful of minutes passed, Corey and Shem reached the valley floor. The ark seemed to grow and become even more colossal. From the east, more animals approached. Now Corey could make out two elephants and two horses.

This was just like the story of Noah and the flood from the Bible. But that wasn't possible, because that happened four thousand years ago.

"Shem?"

"Yes, Corey." The man stopped and so did the male lion. "What troubles you?"

"Where are we going with the lions? And how come there are elephants and horses over there?"

Shem smiled. "Come here, Corey."

Corey led his lion over to Shem. The four stood side by side.

"Not too long ago, the Lord commanded my father to build that boat because soon, raging waters are going to cover this land."

Corey shook his head. How was he here? How was this happening?

Shem continued, "The Lord also commanded that we gather the animals so that they will be saved from the coming flood."

*The great flood? Noah's ark? Impossible!*

Corey looked over and saw two men walking with the elephants and horses. "Are those your brothers?"

"Yes. Ham is the one with the elephants, and Japheth is the man leading the horses. Come! We need to hurry. The Nephilim will surely try to stop us." Shem took off again toward the ark.

Corey started walking, and his lion dutifully followed. He tried to recall what the Nephilim were.

He didn't have to wonder much longer. They hadn't gone twenty paces when Corey saw them. To the west, towering forms lumbered in their direction.

The men had to be at least ten feet tall. Corey counted three men total, with powerful muscles greater than any gym could produce. Huge hands the size of his mother's frying pans. The giants looked like the Hulk minus the green skin. One of the superhumans held some kind of sword that gleamed in the sunlight. The thing looked like a silver surfboard.

He broke from the pack and started running straight for Corey.

# CHAPTER 3

Reality stunned Corey like the big bucket of ice water his buddy dumped over his head last summer. He was soaked in panic as he stared at the leviathan coming toward him.

"Start running!" Shem urged. "Don't fear, brother! The Lord is our shield."

Corey turned around one last time just to make sure his mother and Molly weren't here. They were nowhere in sight. And Corey was still being hunted by a giant man swinging a deadly sword.

Corey started running after Shem and was amazed that the two lions did the same.

The sword-bearing giant closed the gap. He roared some words that Corey didn't understand. Then he boomed, "I WILL DESTROY YOU!"

Even though Corey and Shem were running full speed, there was no way they were going to make it to the boat before the giant predator caught them. And then what? Corey couldn't imagine.

The other two giants joined in the pursuit, running at an angle to cut off Shem and Corey before they reached the ark.

They were trapped.

Shem must have had the same thought. "Stop!"

Corey put on the brakes. The other man and the two lions did the same.

The giant caught up to them and skidded to a halt. The ground quaked. He raised his sword high in the air and brought it down inches away from Corey. The blade pierced the ground all the way to the golden hilt. The other two giants bent down and put their hands on their knees. They stared at their prey with evil eyes.

Both lions began baring their fangs and growling.

"CALM YOUR ANIMALS OR ALL OF YOU GET THE SWORD," the first giant threatened.

Corey watched as Shem stepped forward, in between

the lions and the giant.

"The Lord has commanded that we fill our father's ark with the animals," Noah's son said. "You and your friends can't stop us."

Corey couldn't believe the confidence Shem showed in the face of this crazy situation. He was standing up to a human giant who could pulverize both of them with one hand.

And just like that, one of those hands grabbed Corey and lifted him high in the air. It was like being on a zip line but in reverse. He dangled in the air like a toy in the giant's hand.

That's when he could hear his mother's voice, clear as though she were dangling from the giant's left hand, up in the sky with her boy, high above this bizarre scene.

*"Rely on God. Rely on Him, Corey. He never changes."*

Now was the time to start relying.

"God, please help me!"

Hanging there, Corey noticed that the female lion was inching her body closer to the giant. Then the male lion moved closer. Each crept low, ready to pounce.

"CALL THEM OFF NOW OR—"

The giant didn't get a chance to finish his threat. The lions attacked, each one biting one of the monster's powerful legs. The giant tumbled backward. As his captor fell, he let go of Corey about five feet in the air.

The lions stopped their attack but stayed between the giant and Corey.

"Come, brother!" Shem ran over to help Corey up and make sure he didn't hurt himself in the fall. To the giant he said, "Tell your friends they cannot stand in the way of the Lord's plans. Now leave us!"

Corey watched the giant stand and hobble away on bloody legs. The other two superhumans walked alongside their injured friend. None of the three pulled the sword from the ground.

Corey followed Shem and the lions all the way to the ark. The massive wooden ramp had been lowered, and at the top of it stood an old man with a very long beard.

# CHAPTER 4

"Father, this is my new friend Corey."

"Corey, I'm Noah. Grateful you're here with us." The man shook Corey's hand and gave him a friendly hug, like Corey was part of the family. "There's still a lot of work to do. Shem, put the lions away, and then you can show Corey around."

Noah stepped to the side, and Corey followed Shem into the ark. Cypress wood had been formed into pitch-covered beams and walls to create an engineering masterpiece.

Corey looked up and saw sunlight pour in through a foot-and-a-half opening that ran all around, directly under the massive roof. The natural light illuminated the three main decks of the boat. He was standing in Noah's ark! From where he stood, Corey could see that many wooden stalls were filled with a variety of wild animals. Nearby, two cheetahs rested on a bed of straw, and in a second-level stall, two zebras paced back and forth.

"A little while longer and this place is going to be loaded with animals," Shem said. "The Lord told us to take two of every living creature, male and female."

"Birds, too?"

"Birds, too, and even the reptiles that crawl on the ground. So, Corey, you got here just in time to finish helping us gather all of God's creatures and get them safely on board."

Corey was suddenly overwhelmed with thoughts of his mother. "Can you help me get back home?"

"Where is home, Corey?"

"Texas."

Shem looked confused. "To be honest, I've never heard of that land."

"That's because it hasn't been named yet." Corey tried explaining that he was from four thousand years in the future. But the more he talked, the crazier he sounded. "Never mind."

Shem just smiled and led the two lions into a modest enclosure. He seemed to be considering what Corey had just told him. "You are from the future?"

"I don't understand how I got here, but yes."

Shem rubbed the lions and closed their gate. He turned to look at Corey. "Then you know how all this works out, don't you?"

Corey hesitated. "Yes. I can tell you everything I've read in my Bible."

"That's okay. God commanded this move, so He will see us through. He told my father that He was establishing a covenant with him. God is a promise keeper, Corey. I have faith in His plans for our lives."

Corey thought about his own move and how he didn't want any part of it. He remembered his mother saying they all needed to rely on God because He doesn't change. Four thousand years later, God was leading Corey and his family to a new home. Noah and his family had no idea where they were going, but they knew the One who was calling.

After making sure the lions were secure, Shem led Corey up through the three levels of the ark, past the nervous zebras, a stall with wolves, and even a row of smaller cages filled with cats, rabbits, and badgers. When they reached the upper level, Shem climbed through an open hatch in the roof. He sat down near the edge and invited Corey to sit next to him. The valley stretched out far below them.

Corey took in the panorama and shook his head. He couldn't believe he was on Noah's ark! He still couldn't explain how he got here or how he was getting home.

"Don't worry, Corey. God is taking care of everything. But we have to hurry. See the sky?"

Corey looked up and noticed the sky was dotted with gray clouds. "What on earth were those giants who tried to attack us?"

"They are called Nephilim. Very dangerous. As you saw, they aren't normal humans. They possess superhuman strength. Their size defies explanation. The stories say that they used to be heroes a long time ago. Now they are bent on destruction, but the Lord will protect us. We must have faith."

Corey would be completely satisfied if he never saw another one of the giants ever again.

Noah's son pointed to the west. "Some of the animals are waiting there." Then he pointed to the east. "And the others will come from that direction. We have to finish bringing all of them here before the Lord wipes the land clean. Will you help me, Corey?"

Corey felt stronger sitting next to this man. Being on top of the ark didn't hurt the feeling, either. Here in this place, Corey felt like he had a purpose, and that purpose was directly related to God. "Of course, I want to help."

"It's not going to be easy. There are many more giants. Next time they'll send more than three to try to stop us."

"Well, like you said, God made a covenant with your father."

Shem turned to face Corey. "That's right. We just have to be obedient and not lose faith. No matter how difficult it gets, we must never stop believing that the Lord is who He says He is. Now follow me."

Corey followed the man back down through the ark's multiple levels. As they made their way through the lower deck, Shem stopped to check on the lions. Both were resting and appeared to be recovering from the skirmish with the giants. He grabbed his staff from the floor next to the enclosure and started for the entrance ramp. Ham and Japheth were just finishing with the elephants and horses.

"Come, brothers. Father believes that some of the local villagers are planning on using the Nephilim to steal the animals."

Corey listened, wondering where Shem was headed.

"We're going to find some help." Noah's son offered his staff to Corey.

Corey took the wooden staff, feeling like a track runner in a relay race. He couldn't believe that he was getting to help rescue the animals along with Noah's sons. His heart was filled with courage, and it was a feeling unlike any he'd ever felt before.

He walked down the huge wooden ramp and stared back up into the sky. Many more clouds had formed in the last few minutes. His eyes were probably playing tricks on him. In fact, Corey thought that, just possibly, this whole experience with the ark and Noah was some kind of trick.

But it wasn't. It was real. Just like the coming flood was real.

"I'm proud of you, Corey. You are very brave for someone so young."

Corey did feel brave. He smiled and followed Shem, Ham, and Japheth back out across the valley. Surrounded by these strong men of God, Corey felt like a superhero.

If only his parents were here to see him.

He knew they would be proud of him, too.

# CHAPTER 5

Even more clouds filled the sky now. Corey followed Shem, Ham, and Japheth away from the ark, toward a nearby village on the eastern horizon. They walked in silence for a while, watching the sky lose more light, until they came to a beautiful, ocean-blue river.

"Come, brothers, let us drink before we finish our journey."

Noah's sons knelt down by the water's edge, and using two hands, each scooped up handfuls of water. Corey did the same. The water was surprisingly cold and refreshing.

"There's a man who lives in the village. His name is Ardad. He has been known to talk to the Nephilim."

Corey felt safe with Shem, but didn't know why

he would want to meet with anyone who was an acquaintance of the monsters. Corey took another long drink of water. He wondered how his mother was doing. And Molly.

"He is the only one who hasn't mocked my family for building the ark." Shem got to his feet. "We should go now."

"What do you mean?" Corey asked. He also stood.

Shem pointed back to the ark. "My father never questions the Lord. So when the plans for the ark were shared, there was never any hesitation. He told us God's commands, and we set out to collect the building materials. All the people have called us crazy."

"Except for Ardad?"

Shem smiled. "He is confused, just like the rest of them. But, instead of hurling insults, the man just stares at the ark. It's like his soul is torn. It's like he wants to believe but can't make sense of it all."

"He doesn't have faith," Japheth added.

Ham and Japheth stood, and all the brothers and Corey started walking again. The clouds were definitely getting bigger now. The blue sky was turning black. Shem paused and looked up at the heavens. He considered the clouds. "Do you know what they are?"

"Clouds." Corey couldn't understand how this man had no idea what clouds were. "They usually fill the sky before rain."

"Then it's almost time. We must hurry."

As they quickened their pace, Corey had to ask. "You've never seen clouds before?"

Shem shook his head. "Most of the villagers think my father is missing part of his brain. Can't blame them. When you've never seen rain, then this man starts constructing a gigantic boat. . .well, you get the idea."

Corey understood. This was exactly how he felt about his dad. Corey thought it was foolish that he and his family had to move halfway across the country when they were perfectly fine in Texas. Corey didn't like the unknown. He wanted to reject what he couldn't see, just like all the people living around Noah and his family. They had never experienced rain, so it was just easier to mock the ark and everything it stood for.

Farther along the dirt road, the men saw the outlines of a village. Small mud structures rose above the ground in two rows. The roofs were rounded; they reminded Corey of the bottom side of an egg carton.

As they arrived at the village, Corey watched Shem offer a greeting to a man who sat on the ground near a makeshift gate. He had a full beard and was eating a loaf of bread.

Ham and Japheth nodded at the man. Corey heard them say they were going to split up and question the other villagers. They promised Shem that they would return with information about the Nephilim's plans.

"Meet me back at the ark," Shem said.

"Yes, brother," Ham and Japheth said in unison.

The man named Ardad stopped eating and acknowledged Shem and Corey. "Greetings, son of Noah. Who is your friend?"

"This is Corey."

"Greetings, Corey. Care for bread?"

Shem took Ardad up on the offer.

The villager tore a sizable chunk from his loaf and handed it to Shem. Shem, in turn, broke the chunk in half and gave one portion to Corey. The three ate in silence.

When he finished eating, Shem spoke his reason for the visit.

"We've been loading the ark with animals."

"I saw the lions earlier," said Ardad.

"Then you also saw the Nephilim."

The villager finished his bread and wiped the crumbs from his bushy brown beard. He considered his words before speaking. "I had nothing to do with that, brother."

"That's not why I'm here," Shem replied. "I need your help."

Ardad smiled. "My help? I'm honored."

"Yes. Will you help keep the Nephilim away from us?" Shem offered up the request like it was no big deal. Corey knew from their previous encounter with the giants that what Shem was asking was anything but a small favor.

"And just how do you think I can accomplish that feat? The Nephilim do whatever they want, whenever they want."

Corey watched as Shem knelt down and grabbed a stick. He used it to draw a large circle on the sandy ground. Next, he made a small X in the center of the circle. "Ardad, the X is my father's ark. And here we are." Shem made a second X directly above the first one. "The Nephilim have shelters here and here." Shem added two Xs at the nine and three o'clock positions on the circle.

Corey watched Ardad study the primitive dirt map.

"Those are the two places you are getting the animals from, isn't it?" Ardad asked.

"Yes. If you can keep the Nephilim from this place," Shem said, drawing a vertical line through the top arc of the circle, "then we can get the land animals in from the west. And the mountains that rise in the north will protect our work from the eyes of the Nephilim." Shem added a wide oval in between the X that represented Ardad's village and a vertical line to show the mountains.

"I'll do my best," Ardad said. "When should I start?"

"Now. The sky is changing. You can see it getting darker. Soon it will come."

"Soon what will come?"

"The flood!"

Corey thought he saw Ardad roll his eyes at Shem's mention of the flood. It made Corey think about his conversation with Shem earlier in the day. The part about people thinking Noah was insane. Why would a man build a massive boat just to sit on dry land? Corey knew he would have probably thought the same as Ardad and the rest of the villagers.

Then Corey's thoughts were drawn to Noah. What kind of faith must he have to hear God and obey? To have God tell him that his whole way of living was about to be turned upside down, and still have a faithful heart? Actually, the more he thought about it, this was really similar to Corey's own situation. God was telling Corey that he was moving in much the same way He had told Noah.

"Can I count on you?" Shem's voice broke Corey out of his pondering.

Ardad smiled. "I will try my best. The Nephilim have caused my people harm for a long time, so we will be more than happy to help carry out your request. But, may I give a suggestion?"

Shem nodded.

"The Nephilim go where they want. It might be hard to distract them. But, there are caves high up in the hills along the end of the western path. Bring the animals there to rest and be fed before you take them on to the ark. That will allow you to go back out west for more creatures while my men and I tend to the ones you drop off. The Nephilim don't know about those caves. We use them for shelter."

"Okay, thank you. And thank you for the bread." Shem stood and used his sandal to erase the map he had just drawn.

Ardad stood. When he felt confident there was no sign that a drawing had been made, he said, "Do you want me to find Elizar?"

Shem's calm demeanor went away as fast as the dirt map. "No. We won't resort to his sorcery." He looked up into the cloudy sky. "Let's go, Corey. The animals are waiting."

Corey waved good-bye to Ardad. He walked out of the village with Shem, waiting for the right opportunity to ask who this Elizar was, or if he should even ask at all.

Shem led Corey out the west gate. They noticed Ham and Japheth were there waiting. "How did it go for you, brothers?"

"Shem," said Japheth, "we have to hurry. More

Nephilim are on their way to stop us."

Shem used the stick he was still holding to point in front of them. "There's another village not far down the path. We will look for people who might want to help us keep the Nephilim distracted while we load the animals. But, as my brothers said, we have to hurry."

At the mention of animals, Corey thought about his own dog, Molly. Thinking of Molly made him think about his mother. And thinking of her made him worry about what was going on.

Would he ever see his family again?

# CHAPTER 6

Corey followed all three of Noah's sons out of the village gate. He felt a slight drop in the temperature. The sky was getting darker. The air, colder. Living in Texas, where the weather changed in an instant, helped Corey understand what was happening. A great storm was coming.

"Who's Elizar?"

Shem gave Corey a long look, as if deciding whether to answer the question.

"His name means 'The One Who Deceives.' He uses dark arts to perform magic. You are not the first one to imagine these days, Corey. The people who follow him would say that he is the one who can get you home."

"Get me home?" Corey couldn't believe this strange man might hold the answers to getting him back to his family.

"It's all wrong, brother Corey. I don't know how you got here, or the others before you, for that matter. All I know is Elizar is not the—"

A massive boulder slammed into the path between Corey and the others.

Shouts erupted. Corey missed being pulverized by one short step.

A second boulder slammed into the earth next to the first. Shadows fell with the rocks. Corey looked up and saw giants. Five of them rising above him. Two were empty handed. Three were still holding boulders.

One of the superhumans lifted his burden high above his head and hurled it straight down at Corey. There was no time to think. Corey dived to his right, waiting to be crushed. But the boulder missed its mark and exploded into pieces as it hit another boulder near Corey. He crawled in between the fallen boulders, looking for his friends. Another boulder exploded, raining chunks of rocks over him. And then the last boulder came, slamming into the other boulders.

"Corey, run back to the village. Have Ardad take you back to the ark!" It was Shem's voice.

Corey couldn't leave his new friends. And there was no way he would be able to outrun the giants. Running back to Ardad's village would mean certain doom.

Corey noticed a small arch where a narrow path cut through. It was about a football field away, but if Corey could make it, the Nephilim wouldn't be able to fit. Getting there was the problem.

Five massive superhumans leaned down and began using their gigantic fingers to comb through the rubble looking for Corey. This time there were no animals to help protect him from the monsters. Noah's sons were helpless to keep the giants back. Corey was trapped.

"Run, Corey!" It was Shem again. "Go!"

Corey knew that running was his only choice, even though it didn't seem like a good one. *Just like Dad wanting to move to Florida.* The thought made Corey realize another connection to this Noah's ark world. God met with Noah in the most hopeless situation, the flooding of everything, and made a way out for his salvation.

Corey realized at that moment that his faith had been in himself and what he could or could not do instead of what God could do. *And God can do anything.*

Corey took a deep breath. Exhaled. Each of three of the monsters grabbed one of Noah's sons, while the others moved to intercept Corey. A new blast of cool air came. The storm was still coming. Faster now.

"Shem! I'm heading for that stone arch."

Shem waved at Corey. "Go! The Lord will be with you, child."

*God, forgive me for complaining. You made the universe, so helping me get to that arch is a piece of cake for You.*

Without a care, feeling relieved from finally putting all his trust in God, Corey took off in a full-out sprint for the archway. He thought about his last baseball game, when he was on second with two outs and the score was tied. His friend Riley was up. Riley hit a line drive into right field. Home plate was like the stone arch. Corey had to get there and beat the throw. He remembered rounding third and hearing the screams of all the parents cheering. He remembered seeing the catcher waiting with his glove extended to receive the throw from the outfielder. . . .

The ground shook in his wake, as if Corey were the giant and each of his steps were causing minor earth-quakes. But the tremors came from the pounding of the two giants who were now chasing after Corey. He felt like he was being lifted off the ground in between steps.

Corey kept running. He wanted to look back and check on the brothers, but he couldn't afford to lose time.

There was nothing to hide behind. No weapon to use against the giants. Prayer was his only hope.

One of the attackers lumbered past him and came to a stop between Corey and the arch. Dust rose in thick clouds around the giant's feet and legs. The second giant plodded up behind Corey, trapping him between their towering bodies. More dust was pulled upward in the wake of the giants.

Corey skidded to a stop. He put his hands on his knees and gulped in the dusty air. A wretched cough wracked his throat.

"WHY DO YOU RUN?" the giant in front of Corey boomed. "WHY DO YOU THINK YOU WILL ESCAPE?"

Corey pushed himself back up. He wasn't going to waste his breath answering the giant. He needed all his strength to reach the arch.

*Lord, be with me! Help me get away from these creatures!*

Corey took off at a full sprint, headed straight between the giant's legs.

It was all Corey had left to try. He thought of Noah building the ark and what the man must have thought when God first approached him with the plan to build it. Noah had to think God was missing something obvious. He had to have thought God chose the wrong guy for the job.

Corey made it under the giant but was stopped by a brilliant burst of blue light. Corey staggered as he rubbed his eyes, waiting for his vision to return.

Minutes seemed to pass before Corey could see again. When he could, Corey saw a man wrapped in a hooded black cloak, standing in front of him.

"Greetings, Corey. My name is Elizar. I was told you were asking about me, so I thought it would only be appropriate to introduce myself."

Corey saw the man was holding a staff like Shem's, but his was made of a darker wood. Small wisps of blue light arced from the top of it.

"I'm here to help you. It's obvious you're trapped. But

I want you to know it's because of me that these two giants haven't ripped you to pieces."

Corey remembered Shem had started to say something about not trusting this man. *Lord, help me!* Corey stared at the staff that still had the blue light emanating from the top of it. "I don't need your help."

"I respectfully disagree. Look at you. And the crazy shipbuilder's sons back there. Rather pathetic, I'd say."

Corey just stood there and kept his mouth shut. He had a feeling this guy wasn't done talking.

"Follow me, Corey, and I will show you a life far richer and rewarding than trying to load smelly creatures onto a boat."

Corey stood his ground and remained silent.

"And if that doesn't interest you, how about I get you back home to your mother and Molly? I know they really miss you."

How did he know these things? Yes, Corey did want to get back to his mother and Molly. Yes, he wanted to tell them everything was okay. Maybe testing this man wouldn't hurt.

"How can you get me back?"

The man called Elizar took a step toward Corey. He brought the staff across his chest, holding the dark wood with two hands. "Ah, I didn't think you were interested. Very well. Now that you ask, I have powers that can give you anything you want."

"Leave the boy alone!"

A voice from behind made Corey turn. He saw Ardad coming up quickly.

The dark one spoke again, ignoring the newcomer. "Corey, don't listen to this fool. He has no idea what he's saying."

"Corey, run to the arch!" Ardad was running now.

Elizar took a second step closer to Corey.

"Just follow me, Corey. Let's go see your family."

There was something about the man's soft but commanding voice that drew Corey in.

"Corey!" Ardad had made it and stood next to him. "Don't listen to him. Run!"

The giants hadn't moved.

"There's a reason they haven't moved, Corey. They obey me. They do my bidding. They'll take you home...."

*How does he know what I'm thinking?*

"Run, Corey!"

Corey looked at Ardad. This time the man was carrying a staff. He pointed it toward the stone arch. "Run!"

Corey looked at Elizar. The mysterious man offered Corey a gentle touch on the shoulder. It felt electric. And made Corey afraid. The giants grumbled behind him. More blue light sparked from the end of Elizar's staff.

He didn't think he'd make it to the arch, but Corey felt that was a better option than staying. So he took off running and ran until it felt like his legs were going to explode. As he reached the stone arch, Corey noticed that the path ahead had disappeared.

The giants took off and were right behind him.

There was no choice but to jump out over the abyss.

Corey ran to where the path ended and then kept running, leaping out into air.

And the world fell far away beneath his feet.

# CHAPTER 7

The valley below had a river that cut through it in a wide swath of crystal-blue water. The water expanded as Corey fell down toward it. Cold air raced past him as his body rapidly headed for the ground. He felt like a human roller coaster soaring downhill, trackless and out of control.

A massive wind gust altered Corey's trajectory, pushing him in the direction of the river.

Unlike an Olympic diver, Corey plunged into the river feetfirst. It was a crash landing that afforded no style points but helped him avoid a much more dangerous outcome. The water ripped over him like a liquid blender, twisting Corey's arms and legs into a ball.

When the plummeting came to an end, Corey

pumped back up toward the light. Bursting up through the surface, he gulped in the chilly air and felt the river carry him downstream. He looked up to see one of the giants on the edge of the cliff. Apparently he had no problem navigating the narrow archway. Maybe he had found a way to climb over it. The monster jumped, but his weight prevented him from getting the same air, and he went crashing into the rocks that lined the river's bank.

Corey also saw Ardad running toward the river, his staff raised high above his head.

As Corey treaded water and let the current take him farther downstream, he saw a second giant break through the stone arch and also jump off the cliff. The monster landed on the bank with a sickening thud. Corey was grateful the crash was out of sight. He expected to see Elizar back up on the cliff, but the dark one never appeared again.

Corey wondered what was happening to Noah's sons.

The river picked up speed. White water broke across the surface. A dangerous outcropping of boulders appeared ahead, and Corey was heading straight for it. At that same moment, Ardad was running down the bank with his staff extended out in front of him like he was competing in a pole vault competition. He ran and jumped onto the boulders and waited for Corey. He held his staff out for Corey to grab and used all his strength to pull Corey out of the flowing river.

"We have to hurry and get away from here."

Corey wiped the water from his face and looked at the other man with concern. "What happened to Shem and the others?"

Ardad shook his head. "I'm afraid they are property of the Nephilim now. I have to get you out of here. Elizar will have people waiting for us back at my village. I'm going to take you to a hiding place my people use when they are traveling and want to remain hidden from the Nephilim."

Corey knew there was only one safe place now. "Can't you just take me back to the ark?"

Ardad looked out at the gray horizon. "Elizar will surely try to attack the ark also. We will go and meet up with the others and figure out a plan."

There wasn't time, but Corey needed Ardad's help, so he followed.

ooooo

After a long time of trudging over dirt and sand, Corey and Ardad made it to a remote section of the valley where hills rose up and were covered with caves. Out in the valley, Corey saw a large gathering of all kinds of animals that he hadn't seen before: rhinos, giraffes, gazelles.

"These are the caves I told Shem about. You'll stay here until I can get enough people together to help get you safely back to the ark. In the meantime, you can help take care of the animals. Shem said he'll be back for them soon."

Ardad led Corey into one of the caves that was closest to the ground. Corey was able to stand up as he followed the other man deeper into the cave. Men were there feeding all sorts of wild animals. Corey saw a pair of gorillas and baboons. Next to the primates were smaller creatures that resembled deer. It blew Corey's mind that this diversity of animals was able to be in one place, without walls or any sense of territorial aggression against each other.

"I will be back before long. If Shem and the others arrive before I do, please follow the southern path back to the ark. If not, I apologize in advance for not taking better care of you." The man quickly turned and walked away, disappearing down a dirt path that led to the north.

Corey took a deep breath and exhaled. He was thankful that his life had been spared earlier, when the dark one tried to capture him.

His attention was taken by two majestic jaguars that were standing close by. Their golden eyes seemed to glow in the dim cave. They started rubbing against Corey's legs. It was like they were wanting to get out. Without thinking, he guided the jaguars down the side of the hill and then to the path and helped them join the other animals waiting in the valley. Hopefully, Shem and the other brothers would find a way to elude the monsters and take them to the ark before it was too late. Corey ran back up the hill toward the safety of the caves.

ooooo

First came a burst of electric blue light. Then Ardad stepped from the shadows. Coming out directly behind him was the mysterious man wrapped in the dark cloak, dark staff held high. Blue light spitting out from the end.

What was Elizar doing here? Ardad was clear in his

directions to Corey about waiting in the cave. Corey should have obeyed, but he wanted to help the jaguars. Besides, he was only away from the caves for a few minutes.

"I'm sorry, Corey. I had no choice. He was going to hurt my family if I didn't tell him where I'd taken you."

So, this had nothing to do with Corey. Ardad had only wanted Corey to stay in the cave because he wanted him there when Elizar returned. Corey had never experienced betrayal before.

*"For all the people on earth had corrupted their ways."*

Corey remembered the Bible said that Noah walked faithfully with God but that the world had become full of violence.

Even people who acted like friends didn't care about one another.

The dark one came forward to collect Corey. The rest of the animals didn't stir or growl in disapproval of what was happening. "You should have joined me when I extended an invitation."

A giant lumbered out from the shadows and lifted Corey off the ground. There was no use fighting. Corey was trapped. The Goliath carried Corey away from the animals, out across the plains, and on to a remote stretch of land that was filled with what looked to be holes in the ground.

Elizar appeared, seemingly out of nowhere again, and this time his voice was completely devoid of compassion. "Put him in."

The giant carrying Corey moved closer to one of the holes and lifted him over it. Corey could see in the fading light that the thing was wide and deep enough to drop a person in. Which is exactly what the giant did.

Unlike the river, there was no water to break Corey's fall.

# CHAPTER 8

Corey landed on a bed of sticks and straw. He had to be at least twenty feet down. Despite the night, darkness seemed to thicken. Corey pushed himself to stand but soon realized he was trapped. There was no way out of the deep cistern.

Corey tried in vain to scale the dirt walls but found nothing to hold on to. Each time he made an effort to pull himself up, chunks of dirt came loose, sending him back to the bottom of the well.

He sat down and stared up at the sky. Tiny droplets of water began to land on his face. The great storm was coming. And, given his current situation, Corey figured that the floodwater would eventually fill the giant hole, thereby lifting Corey out. There was nothing to worry about. Just wait. And wait some more.

Not much time passed before an animal's face appeared over the edge of the cistern. It belonged to a massive cat. Even in the fading light, Corey could make out the light brown fur and white mouth. A cougar.

He knew these animals from schoolbooks, but Corey felt like he had been connected to them for a long time. Even though it had only been hours since he arrived in this alternate world, Corey came to think of the animals as good friends.

A second animal came into view next to the cougar. Corey knew this animal was a lynx by its large pointed ears that had black tufts of fur sticking out.

A third cat appeared. This one looked like a bobcat. Corey saw the long whiskers and the fur on the face resembling a beard.

A fourth was a cheetah.

Next came a regal tiger.

Then a puma.

Seventh, and last to join the ring of animals that were watching over Corey, was a beautiful creature with gray-and-tan fur and hypnotizing green eyes. A snow leopard. This last cat turned to grab something with its powerful jaws. When the cat lifted its head back over the cistern, Corey noticed that it was holding a thick stick in its mouth.

The cat flicked its head up and let go of the stick. When it dropped to Corey, he didn't know whether to feel joy or sadness. The stick was actually a staff. Shem's to be exact. Corey could tell from the markings on the hook.

No sooner did Corey feel relief from having the staff as a connection to Shem and the brothers than a new wave of darkness came. The seven animals scattered. Their heads disappeared from view and were replaced by a black cloak blending with the night.

Elizar.

No words were spoken. As fast as the dark one appeared, he vanished. In his place came one of the giants carrying a large wooden grate. The monster-human dropped it across the hole, trapping Corey deep inside.

*When the flood comes, I won't be able to get out.*

No more animals came. No more people. No more giants.

The only thing that came was more darkness. Waves and waves of darkness crashing over Corey as he fell into a fitful sleep.

# CHAPTER 9

When Corey opened his eyes, the animals were gone. He still held Shem's staff, and he was still at the bottom of a very deep well. The wind grew stronger, blowing big gusts down over him. Heavy drops of water splattered over his face and arms.

The flood was coming to wipe everything away, and the worst part was that Corey wouldn't get out alive.

He was trapped.

The heavy beams of wood that formed the grate still covered the cistern, keeping Corey in like a prisoner held against his will.

The rain felt like it was falling harder now, soaking Corey's clothes and hair. The dirt walls were slowly melting into mud. Helplessness fell over Corey, mixed with the rain. Now, stuck in this dark place, all he wanted was to be free. Here in the well, all Corey could think about was the end. . .when the floods came and he would surely drown.

Right now the fear of the Florida move seemed ridiculous. Corey was ashamed of himself that he ever once complained. Right now, practically buried in the earth, Corey couldn't help but admit his selfishness.

"Lord Jesus, forgive me."

Abandoned.

Alone.

Afraid.

"Please help me, Jesus."

Corey's mind went haywire, overloading with a mixture of panic and selfish pride. He was scared and didn't want to die, but he didn't believe that his life could actually be almost over. His parents always told him he was special. They always made him feel like a king. Except, the truth was, here in this wherever-he-was place—this bizarre dreamscape—Corey was nothing. He always thought bad things happened to other people. Now the bad things were all his.

"Jesus, help me."

But Corey needed a miracle, and none seemed to be coming. Lying there in the muddy water, hopelessly trapped at the bottom of a nondescript well, Corey doubted. He doubted that God was there with him. He doubted and felt terrible for it.

"God, forgive me."

More rain.

More doubting.

More shame.

The shame made Corey think about a story his New York grandpa always told. It was the best story he had ever heard his grandfather share. There was something about it that made Corey know that God really did forgive sins and selfishness.

ooooo

When Opa, Corey's great-grandfather in New York, first came to America as a young man, he had sailed across the Atlantic with other immigrants from Germany. Arriving at Ellis Island and seeing the Statue of Liberty filled Grandpa with awe. He admitted to Corey that he'd been scared to move halfway around the world to the United States, but he had hope that moving meant having a new chance for a better life.

Needing money, Opa landed a job as a short-order cook at Vinnie's, a hole-in-the-wall diner on Manhattan's Lower West Side. Opa flipped hamburgers and crafted BLTs for Wall Street suits who lived in a constant state of hustle. The silver order wheel was always filled with slips: hash browns, eggs, bacon, sausage, grilled cheese, fried bologna. It was grueling work standing over a hot stove all day, but Opa believed in doing his best even in hard times.

There was never a day when he messed up an order. All those days. All those customers. All those orders. Not a single mistake.

Until the afternoon that John Ride came back.

Opa knew the man by heart. The two had met during Grandpa's first days at the diner. John Ride was big. Tall and strong. He looked like he could rip a phone book in half with his bare hands. That was way back in the days before phones became smart.

The mistake happened when Opa grabbed the next batch of tickets off the wheel and read them. The diner was packed with the typical lunch crowd. Private conversations mingled with waitresses calling out special requests to Opa behind the counter. He kept looking at the towering form of John Ride. Great-grandpa set the tickets down and started preparing three hamburger patties for the grill. The problem was the tickets were for three ham sandwiches.

Opa never thought he'd see Mr. Ride again. At their first meeting, Mr. Ride had sat at the counter. He ordered coffee, no cream or sugar. No food.

This second encounter, Mr. Ride ordered the exact same thing. Coffee. No cream or sugar. Opa heard his voice over the cacophony of diner sounds. "Is Henry here?" The waitress said, "Of course, honey. Hold your horses while I go get him."

Opa had no choice but to face his past and greet Mr. Ride. After all those years.

He wiped his hands on his apron and stepped out of the kitchen.

"Henry," the giant customer said. "It's been a while."

Great-grandpa knew he had to apologize for the past. His past. His past shame was being offered a chance to seek forgiveness.

"John. . .I'm so sorry." Opa looked at the floor between them. "Please forgive me."

The big man pulled an envelope out of his jacket pocket and put it on the counter next to his coffee cup. "Henry, by God's grace, I forgave you a long time ago. Today, I came back to show you I mean it." Ride pushed the envelope across the bar. "Take it."

Out of respect, Opa took the envelope.

"Open it, Henry." Mr. Ride took a sip of his coffee. He had the smile of parents who are watching their child open a big gift on Christmas morning.

Opa opened the envelope. Inside he found ten one-hundred-dollar bills and a note: *Jesus loves you, Henry. He is NOT ashamed of you. John 3:16*

Opa lost the fight to hold back his tears. He used the greasy apron to wipe his wet face. When he dropped the apron, Ride was gone.

That night Opa went home holding on to the envelope like it was something sacred. He fell to his knees and asked Jesus to forgive his heart problem. He asked Jesus in. To take over. Right then he promised his Savior that he would use every penny of that money for good.

ooooo

Corey recalled that story every time he felt like he had made one too many mistakes to be forgiven. Sitting in the well, armed only with Shem's staff and no way out, Corey asked Jesus to forgive his complaining and ungrateful heart. He knew Jesus did. He knew Jesus erased the shame Corey felt from his own selfishness.

He felt the rain. It kept coming, just like the truth found in Opa's story. Corey remembered asking him what he did wrong.

He answered, "Corey, I am ashamed of myself. That first time John Ride ate at Vinnie's, he left his wallet on the counter. I took it to hold on to so no one would steal it. I counted the money in it. Sixty dollars, which is about a thousand dollars today. Days passed, and Ride never came back asking for the wallet. I knew I should just hold on to it, but I didn't. Money was tight, and I needed to pay my rent. I was behind so I used all of Ride's money.

"The very next day after I spent the money, Ride came in the diner looking for his wallet! He asked for me personally. I lied and told him I never saw it. He looked at me long and hard, even gave a faint smile—like he knew I had his money—thanked me, and just walked out."

∞∞∞

Corey also remembered how his great-grandfather kept the promise. He converted the thousand dollars that Ride brought back in the envelope into ten-dollar bills and gave it all away to the homeless. Opa kept track of the hundred names he gave the money to and prayed over them. He broke up the blessing and multiplied it.

Here in the well, Corey couldn't find the blessing. He was at the end where blessings aren't found.

# CHAPTER 10

Rain continued to fall from the sky.

Fifteen feet above, Corey saw movement, like shadows sweep across the grate.

The shadows kept sweeping back and forth across the opening, and finally Corey could see that the shadows were actually two elephant trunks. They both began to curl around one of the heavy crossbeams. The trunks went taut. The elephants were trying to pull the grate away!

Corey watched in awe as the mighty trunks pulled the grate loose with ease.

Now the problem for Corey was getting himself out of the well, armed only with Shem's staff. He thought about his grandfather's story again.

The blessing was the animals removing the barrier. But there had to be something else. All Corey had was the staff. He thought hard about his situation. How could the staff help him get out of the well?

*Break up the blessing. Multiply it.*

The only thing Corey could think of was to break the staff in half. He brought the staff down over his left thigh and snapped the wood in two. Each end tapered into a point. Corey reached as high as he could and shoved one of the pointed ends into the cistern wall. Corey pulled up on that pole and then with his left hand shoved the other staff piece a little farther up the well wall.

The muddy walls received the staff with hardly any resistance. After a couple of times repeating this pull/shove motion, Corey could barely hold his weight. He managed to pull himself halfway up the well, but he didn't have the power to go any higher. Suspended there, Corey prayed that he wouldn't let go, because if he fell back to the bottom, there was no getting out.

Arms burning, Corey called out for help. He hoped Shem or one of Noah's other sons could hear. But no one came.

Corey felt something brush against his hair. He looked up and saw that one of the elephants was dangling its trunk over him. Then the second trunk appeared. Corey knew he'd have only one shot of letting go of the staff pieces and grabbing the trunks.

His arms were burning.

*Lord, please help me!*

Corey reached out with his right hand to grab the closer trunk. He couldn't get his hand around it to get a good grip. He couldn't hang on anymore with his left hand. He let go of the staff and started falling.

The second trunk rose and caught him. It wrapped around his stomach. Both trunks lifted Corey all the way up and out of the well! They put him down carefully on the ground next to the opening. Even though his muscles were on fire, Corey rejoiced that he had been set free.

As he sat there catching his breath, a pair of rhinos lumbered forward. The creatures were so huge and intimidating. Corey remembered reading that a male rhino could weigh up to five thousand pounds and charge at up to speeds of thirty-five miles per hour.

But Corey wasn't afraid, because for some reason the

animals here were loving and tame.

"Praise the Father, you're okay!"

Corey saw his friend step from the shadows.

"Shem!"

"We have to hurry. The Nephilim will soon return. Come, use that boulder to climb onto the rhino's back. Like this. . ."

Corey watched the man effortlessly climb from the rock to the animal. Shem straddled the creature and then waved for Corey to do the same.

When Corey got up on the rhino, he couldn't believe that he was actually sitting on the back of such a powerful beast.

"Hold on, brother!"

# CHAPTER 11

It took a handful of strides for the rhinoceros to get moving, but when it did, Corey couldn't believe the feeling. He was being carried across the wide-open valley just as if he were riding a horse back home in Texas.

The animal's wide back provided enough room for Corey to feel confident that he wouldn't fall off. The tough leather hide rippled from the mighty muscles pumping up and down. Shem was on the other rhino right behind him.

Corey felt like he was flying! As he looked around, he saw that many other animals had joined the journey. Tigers, gazelles, giraffes. Even the two elephants that had helped Corey escape from the well were now part of the group. It was like one of those African safaris Corey had seen on the Internet.

So many animals. No predators. No prey. All simply running together. It was magical.

Corey couldn't believe he was really riding on the back of a massive, thundering rhino. The hills and trees flew by and the air rushed across his face.

"WHERE ARE WE GOING?" Corey yelled over to Shem. The man looked just as excited as Corey to be careening over the landscape on the broad back of a rhinoceros.

"I WANT TO SHOW YOU SOMETHING UN-BELIEVABLE!" Shem yelled from behind him.

The rhino soon found a rocky path that narrowed as it made its way up from the valley, higher and higher into the hills. Corey turned his head and could see that Shem and the second rhino were close behind. The other animals broke away and headed farther down the valley toward the ark.

Eventually the path ended. The two rhinos skidded to a stop, very close to the edge of a cliff that overlooked the valley.

Corey was mesmerized by the weather. The view from

high on top of this hill was breathtaking. It looked like a Fourth of July spectacular. Lightning exploded across the dark sky like fireworks. The electric light display was amazing. Bolts of white and blue made jagged paths across the heavens. Epic strikes ripped in a thousand random directions. Like God was drawing in the sky.

"It's as if the Father is giving a final sign to the people." Shem pointed up to the sky. "A beautiful display of His power for the villagers who have thought my family were wild people all these days."

Cold air swirled over Corey, and he shivered. The temperature was dropping. The epic storm was getting closer and closer. Time was running out.

"Shem, would your father let anyone on the ark?"

"Of course, brother Corey. But as I've said before, all the villagers think he is nothing more than a fool. They refuse to believe."

Another round of lightning arced throughout the sky. White lines zigzagged from the sky toward the ground in brilliant bursts of energy. Clouds were gathering high above them like spectators waiting to cheer on the approaching flood.

"Brother, the clouds," Shem noted as he pointed to the towering gray sky.

"Yes, clouds."

Corey nodded. He held back a chuckle as he recalled his earlier conversation with Shem about the weather. It was still hard to imagine that it had never rained here before. So, of course, Noah and his family would never have witnessed clouds and the rains.

"Clouds. Wonderful creation. Clouds hold the rain, you said?"

Now Corey couldn't hold back the smile. "Yes, Shem, the clouds hold the rain."

The lightning seemed to intensify as new bolts shot in every direction, illuminating the evening sky.

Noah's son stared at the heavenly display, enthralled by the beauty and intensity of it all.

Corey kept his eyes on the show but had a question for his friend. "How did you and your brothers escape Elizar?"

"Just like you, we had help. From the animals."

"But I had your staff. How did you call them?" It was hard for Corey to concentrate on the conversation and the feeling he had from his first rhino ride. And the lightning above. And the coming flood. It was all so overwhelming.

"The staff I gave you was my father's. He was the one who brought the elephants from the other side of the valley to the ark. Ham slipped away from the Nephilim and made it back to tell Father we needed the elephants to get you out."

From their high place on the cliff, Corey saw the animals that had been running with them made it safely to the ark.

"I could stay and watch this forever, but we must get back." Shem used his legs to signal his rhino to turn back toward the path.

Corey tried nudging his rhino to do the same, but his didn't budge.

"Kick harder! Trust me, you won't hurt him." Now Shem was the one who was smiling.

Corey mustered all the strength he could and kicked the animal with his legs. The rhino stirred and finally began to move toward Shem and the other rhino.

"There you go. Now follow me!"

Corey loved the experience of riding this powerful creature back down the narrow path. As they rode, the lightning kept exploding across the sky, high above them.

As they were approaching the bottom of the path, where it met the valley, two Nephilim were waiting. Each held a massive club that looked to Corey like the trunks of two old oak trees.

"RAM THEM, COREY!"

Corey watched Shem kick his rhino. Corey did the same. Both animals picked up speed and charged the giants with their horns out to attack.

Corey felt like the giants were going to smash them and the rhinos into the future with those clubs.

When Corey and Shem were about thirty feet away, the giants lifted their clubs just as Corey feared.

And the clubs came down at them like they were baseballs served up perfectly over the middle of the plate.

"JUMP!"

Shem briefly stood on the back of his rhino before launching himself off the right side of the animal. The club missed its mark, but the charging rhino did not. Its horn rammed straight into the closest giant's knee, causing him to fall like a bowling pin.

Corey managed to push himself to his knees. The second giant was already swinging his club. Corey jumped. As he went airborne, Corey saw that his rhino's horn also connected. The second giant went down just like the first one did.

Corey landed on his feet, but because of the speed, he barrel-rolled through the tall grass that bordered the path. As he stood and got his bearings, Corey noticed that Shem was standing over him.

"You are strong, young man! Don't ever fear. Now we must hurry."

"Not so fast!" The voice belonged to the wicked Elizar. "I will be joining you on the ark."

# CHAPTER 12

The dark one moved toward Corey as more Nephilim came over the crest of the surrounding hills. The two giants who had been toppled by the rhinos had gotten back on their feet and trudged up on either side of Elizar.

Shem started running and Corey followed, but a row of giants blocked their path.

"It's no use, son of Noah. If you really believe that your father is following directions from God, then you'll listen to me. Carefully."

More of the mighty Nephilim came forward and circled around Corey and Shem. There were no animals around to save them. Now they were completely at the mercy of the one called Elizar.

"I want a place on that thing you call an ark. I

want my people to have a place, too. These wild things happening in the heavens are obvious signs from the gods."

Corey looked at Shem, then at Elizar. Even the giants held his attention. There wasn't any way out.

Shem looked at the one cloaked in black and, as he began to speak, pointed at the roiling sky. "The ark is there because my father believes in the one true God. You and everyone else laughed at him. Now that you see the end is near, you have a change of heart?"

Before Elizar could offer a reply, more movement came at the top of the hill. Now Corey saw a huge wave of people walk over it and come to stand behind Elizar. Ardad was part of the crowd. He came up and stood beside the dark one. His eyes locked onto Corey's.

Elizar continued his speech. "I do not have to justify my words or actions to someone like you or your peasant family for that matter. You, however, have to do what I say or there will be a massive problem."

Shem ignored the threat. "Come on, brother Corey."

"TAKE HIM!"

One of the giants bent down and grabbed Corey.

"Shem, son of Noah, I will take the boy's life if you disobey. Now walk ahead of us and tell that father of yours to let us board."

Shem tossed the staff he'd been carrying up to Corey. Then he closed his eyes.

"Shem, go now or the boy won't be alive to help anymore."

Shem took off running across the valley toward the ark.

Corey hung suspended in the air and saw Elizar step closer. The world was about to flood, and Corey wouldn't be on the ark.

At least he could see in the distance that Shem was almost to the boat. The last of the animals were walking up the huge wooden ramp.

Still hanging in the air, Corey tried to push away the reality that this was how he was going to die.

This was the end.

# CHAPTER 13

A thunder of a hundred storms boomed over the valley, causing the ground to shift. More thunder. More shifting. The earth began to crack.

To catch his fall, the giant had to drop Corey.

The ground had not shaken under the weight of the Nephilim.

It seemed to have come from underneath Corey's feet, from somewhere deep within the earth. Ardad looked like he had just received the worst news of his life.

But maybe a group of giants had fallen and Corey just missed it. He turned to survey the valley.

There were no signs that the giants had any men down. But what Corey did see were massive cracks ripping across the ground. It was as if the ground were made from paper and some invisible hand was tearing it up. Ardad's face was now the reflection of total fear. The villagers who had come in Elizar's defense were now running for their lives.

And then the whole world shifted again. The ground pulsed upward and threw Corey on his back. It took a second to realize boulders the size of cars were rolling straight at him. More earth exploded, sending dirt flying over him. It was getting hard to breathe or see. But, through it all, Corey managed to hold on to the new staff Shem had given him.

And then came the water! Massive geysers blew hundreds of feet in the air, up through cracks in the surface. Water sprayed over Corey, making it nearly impossible for him to get his bearings. He thrashed and flailed against nature's fury until he could finally stand on his feet.

But he was no sooner standing than he looked out and saw something more ominous than the rising waters. It was more frightening than the idea of moving to a new state or a hundred nightmares rolled into one.

Elizar and the entire Nephilim army.

Evil backed by more evil.

And then, with a shattering boom, the giant army attacked. Corey had nowhere to go.

He yelled out for the Lord to intervene.

The first one to reach him was Elizar. He looked at Corey and grimaced. "I'm impressed that you made it this far. I thought you'd perish back in the well."

Corey searched for a way out, but there wasn't one. His brain sounded the panic bells.

In just seconds, the enemy's soldiers would extinguish Corey like a dying flame.

Where was his mother? His dog, Molly? He wanted to see them one last time.

"But," Elizar said, "you've proved no different than the fool and his ark-building, animal-loving family."

The Nephilim joined their grunts and yells into a venomous chorus.

"TEAR HIM APART!"

"RIP HIS LIMBS OFF!"

"THROW HIM INTO THE ABYSS!"

Corey refused to stand there and do nothing. He ran

straight at Elizar. The man's face changed from a mocking smile to a concerned glare. Corey swung the staff at the man, surprising himself at how much adrenaline was racing through his system. The staff connected with Elizar's left knee like it was a slider, pitched low and outside.

More fountains of water blew up through the earth, spouting like supernatural geysers trying to spray the heavens with their powerful might. A wave swept Corey and Elizar off their feet and carried them about two hundred yards away from the giants. As fast as it came, the mighty wave receded.

"Corey," Elizar yelled, "you can't beat me! My master's army is too powerful for a little boy like you."

Corey looked past the man and saw the giants jumping into the growing current. They were trying to reach Corey and teach him a lesson about not obeying Elizar.

Corey prayed out loud again. "Father God, please save me!"

Elizar got to his feet and stood over Corey. "It doesn't look like your God is listening, does it?"

Corey, still on his back, clothes drenched from the

growing flood, looked at the evil man standing over him. He considered his words. It certainly felt to Corey like he was alone and God was somewhere far away.

"Corey, all I need from you is that staff Shem gave you. Just hand it over, and I will be on my way."

The flood story was clear. The world was destroyed, and everyone perished except for Noah and his family. Corey still couldn't understand why he was here, experiencing all this, but he was deciding right at this moment to trust God to see him through. "I'm not giving you the staff."

The earth rocked back and forth beneath them. New cracks exploded open all around them. More towers of water rocketed toward the dark sky. It was all Corey could do to keep his hands clenched tightly to the wooden staff.

The Nephilim had made it through the churning tide to Elizar. They climbed out of the water and stood on either side of the man cloaked in black. They fixed their hideous eyes on Corey.

"Young man, don't be ridiculous. You can see we are more powerful. You are outnumbered and hopeless. And it is clear your God isn't coming to save you."

As the last word came from Elizar's mouth, another blast of water shot up from behind Corey. The ground beneath his back gave way, and he felt himself falling. The ground had been torn in two. He could see Elizar and the giants, but they were still high up on the cliff. Corey kept falling until finally, he plunged into a body of water. The force of hitting the swirling sea dazed Corey. He didn't know which way was up. His body was being yanked under. Water kept spraying in his mouth, making it harder to breathe. His lungs started to burn.

One of the giants who had been mocking Corey back on the cliff threw a log at him. The wooden missile plunged into the water mere feet away from Corey. He managed to reach out and grab the wood with one hand, still not letting go of the staff. Temporary relief came as the current carried the boy and the beam farther away from the evil ones.

Corey felt fear wash over him, as real as the waves that moved his feeble body up and down, up and down. All he wanted to do was see his mother and Molly. He called their names, but they didn't answer. The wind blew fierce, like a thousand wolves howling at a thousand moons.

On the horizon, the immense ark was being carried away. The old man and his family had no idea the boy was dying.

Corey couldn't think straight. His body was broken, and his brain was shutting down. He tried to figure out a way to save himself, but there was none.

A wall of water slammed over Corey, ripping the log from his grip. The rain poured down in golf ball–sized drops. It rattled Corey's face and head.

Through the watery haze, Corey could see the giant pick up another log and hurl it down at him.

The water was pulling the ark away into darkness.

And it was doing the same to Corey. . . .

# CHAPTER 14

The raging water lifted Corey up and then brought him crashing down. He braced for the feeling of being pummeled by the log, but it never came.

Elizar and his evil army of giants weren't so lucky. As the rain fell, huge drops splattering over Corey and the newly formed sea, he couldn't believe his eyes. The entire cliff came crashing down into the churning waters.

Elizar and the Nephilim all fell into a watery grave. But there was no time to celebrate, because Corey had to make it to the ark.

Corey had somehow managed to hold on to the staff. But it was getting hard to concentrate on holding on to the log, too. At least the current was carrying him straight toward the ark, because there was no way he could steer. Corey was at the mercy of the flood.

Hanging on with all the strength that remained, he let the current carry him toward the massive ark. He was headed straight for it. Within minutes he was going to be rescued, and all of this would be over.

He saw the old man, Noah, standing on the plank waiting with outstretched arms to receive Corey and pull him to safety. Corey was so close.

But just before he reached the ark, something yanked on his leg and sucked him under.

A powerful hand gripped his leg—the giant hand of one of the Nephilim was holding him down below the water. Corey couldn't hold his breath much longer. He said a final silent prayer.

His lungs were on fire. He knew as soon as he opened his mouth, the water would rush in and put out that fire, but it would also put out his life. He couldn't think. He lost all control of his arms and legs. He felt the staff being tugged away.

But just as his brain commanded his mouth to open, Corey felt his body being pulled up out of the water. A blurry form had lifted him up by the other end of the staff.

Cool air blew all around him. He breathed the life-giving oxygen in. . .deep, and it was good.

The next things he heard were voices calling his name.

Was he in the ark, safe from the Nephilim?

One of the voices sounded familiar. It was soft and sweet and sounded just like his mother.

# CHAPTER 15

## PRESENT DAY
## THREE MONTHS LATER

### CLEARWATER, FLORIDA

The Gulf of Mexico reached out to the horizon like a deep blue field of hope. An orange setting sun cast glittering light across the scene. Corey couldn't believe how incredible God's design was. The vast waters made him flash back to the great flood experience. Many times since the move from Texas to Florida, Corey wondered what it all meant.

Watching Molly jump through the crashing waves made Corey smile. His dog snapped at the white foam and barked an unknown message to the surf. Corey thought whatever it was, Molly was happy.

Things did have a way of working out, because just like his dog, Corey was happy and had to admit that moving halfway across the United States to Florida wasn't at all like he expected. In the three short months that he had been here, Corey made new friends and was adjusting to his new school.

The best part of the move so far was that his new house was literally a block away from the beach. His mom made a deal with him that if he kept a good attitude about things, she would bring him and Molly to the beach after school. It was amazing to be able to come out on the sand and run through the water anytime he wanted.

And then there was his new friend Noah. God surely had a sense of humor there, because Noah's dad was a fisherman and owned a big boat that he took the boys on just last week. Noah was turning eleven today, and his pirate-themed birthday party was starting here on the beach with a scavenger hunt for buried treasure.

"Hey, Corey!"

Corey turned and saw his new friend waving. Noah had his favorite Tampa Bay Buccaneers shirt on. He loved the logo: tattered red battle flag with a skull and crossed swords. Noah sketched it in class any chance he could get. That's why Corey had no problem picking out a present: a Bucs football with the logo printed on one side and the NFL lettering on the other.

"Hey!" Corey handed Molly off to his mother and then jogged over to Noah. He handed Noah his present.

"Thanks! Come on. We're starting off up on the pier. My uncle Mike is pretending to be a pirate. He's going to hand us treasure maps and give us an idea where the loot is hidden."

Corey followed his friend down the shore to the fishing pier. The boys hurried up the wooden stairs and through the bait shop to the other side where Noah's uncle waited in his full pirate regalia.

After giving each of them a rolled-up piece of manila paper, Pirate Mike told the boys that their map would help them find the buried treasure, which included everything from a video game to actual money. "If you're not finding anything," Uncle Mike added, "come get me. I'll be over there by the sand dunes watching the sunset."

The boys took off running back out through the bait shop and down to the beach. They all wanted the video game. But Noah stayed behind. He smiled at Corey.

"What's up?" Corey asked.

"My parents came up with the idea of giving me a different map than everyone else. Most of the good stuff is on my map."

"Cool. Where do we start?"

Noah unrolled his map and scanned it. "Looks like the best loot is over that way by the dunes."

Corey gave his friend a thumbs-up.

"My mom said she was bringing Hunter. I'm gonna see if they're here yet!"

Corey's heart went out to his friend. Noah told him the story how he had been playing with his two dogs, Hunter and Sky, last Friday. Noah's dad threw the tennis ball over the fence. And when Noah went to grab it, he came back in their yard but forgot to close the gate. That night, after Noah had gone to bed, his mother let the dogs out. Sky never came back.

Noah couldn't bear the guilt. His parents couldn't console him. But for some reason, Noah talked to Corey.

"Hey, I see my mom!" Noah climbed up on the railing

to get a better view of the parking lot. He leaned out to wave at his mother.

"What's up?"

"My mom's got Hunter! I see—"

Then time seemed to slow to a sickening pace. Corey watched in disbelief as his friend lost balance and fell forward, out over the railing. Down into the ocean.

"No!" Corey yelled but then heard—

"Corey! Help me!"

What?

Noah hadn't fallen into the water!

Not yet.

He'd reached out, managed to grab the pier, and was hanging by one hand.

Corey dropped to his knees. "Noah! Grab my hand!"

The boy's eyes were wide from fear. "Help me, Corey! Please, help me!"

Corey lay flat on his stomach and grabbed his friend's arm. "I've got you, Noah!" But the weight began pulling down harder than Corey could pull up. Soon, Noah would have to let go and Corey would have to watch. Then his friend would hit the churning water and soon be taken down into its watery depths.

"I've got you!"

But not for long.

A man who had been fishing turned and saw the two boys. He dropped his pole on the pier and ran over to help. The fisherman knelt down and grabbed Noah's arm. "Okay, got him!"

Corey let go of his friend's arm and moved back. He watched the man pull Noah up onto the pier.

"Thanks, Corey. You saved me!"

Corey couldn't believe the similarities to his own experience with the flood. He had just saved his new friend from falling into the water. All he needed now was to see an ark floating on the Gulf. . .

The fisherman helped the boys walk back down the wooden steps of the pier. They made their way across the warm white sand toward the parking lot.

Noah looked up and saw his mother was now walking *two* dogs. Both golden retrievers.

"Sky?"

Noah's mother unleashed the dogs. Both ran right for Noah. Corey waited a few steps back to let his friend embrace the moment.

"Sky!" Noah hugged his dogs and looked at his mother, who had knelt down in the sand by her son. "How?"

Noah's mother reached out and put one hand on her son and the other on the retriever. "Turns out a family on the other side of our neighborhood found her Friday night. They took her in and loved on her, but didn't see our sign until yesterday. I asked if she could stay there last night so we could surprise you today."

Corey knew the feeling his friend had in his heart. The one where you know you are blessed. The one that's indescribable because words can't define the emotions. Just as Noah thought that his dog was gone forever, only to now hug her again. Just as Corey thought that moving to Florida was going to be a nightmare, only to now meet his new friend.

His mom was right. Things change.

But God doesn't.

Corey stood back and watched his friend get covered in hugs and kisses, from both his animals and his parents.

He imagined God doing the same for all His children.

Corey finally understood how much God loved him.

He closed his eyes and felt the sun on his back.

*Thank You, Lord.*

*Thank You.*